Tonka

W9-DIN-974

WORKING THE FARM

by Mara Conlon
Illustrated by Jesus Redondo

No part of this publication may be reproduced, stored in a retrieval system, or transmitted in any form or by any means, electronic, mechanical, photocopying, recording, or otherwise, without written permission of the publisher. For information regarding permission, write to Scholastic Inc., Attention: Permissions Department, 557 Broadway, New York, NY 10012.

HASBRO and its logo and TONKA are trademarks of Hasbro and are used with permission.
© 2013 Hasbro. All rights reserved.

Published by Scholastic Inc., 557 Broadway, New York, NY 10012. SCHOLASTIC and associated logos are trademarks and/or registered trademarks of Scholastic Inc.

ISBN 978-0-545-55026-0

12 11 10 9 8 7 6 5 4 3 2 1 13 14 15 16 17/0
Printed in the U.S.A. 40
First printing, September 2013

SCHOLASTIC INC.

A  is a busy place for trucks.

A  uses trucks to help him grow

crops like  ,  , and  vines.

Tonka
Tonka
Tonka
Tonka

This  is bringing beehives to the orchard. The bees carry pollen to the  on the  . This helps the  grow.

Tonka

When the  are ripe, the 

goes to work. The  picks the 

off the  . He puts them in  .

The  will carry the  to a

cooler for storage.

Tonka
Tonka

A  also does a lot of work on a  . In the spring, the  uses a powerful  to plant different kinds of  . The  pulls a row planter through the fields. The row planter drops  into the soil.

Tonka

The  grow into tall stalks of  . Then the  uses a  to cut and gather the  . The  removes the husks from the ears of  . Harvesting is a big job, and the  does important work on a  .

Tonka

Trucks do a lot of different jobs

on a  . This  is so large,

the  can't lift it! Instead, he uses

a  to pick up the giant 

and move it across the  .

Tom

The trucks on this  also help

the  care for his animals. The  ,

 , and  on the  eat

 . This big forage harvester

chops  into small pieces.

The  is turned into  for

the animals to eat.

Tonka
Tonka
Tonka

A  squeezes the  together

to form stacks or bales.  bales

can be round or square. Then a

 picks up the stacks of 

and carries them to the  .

Tonka

Today, the  is getting ready for some special visitors. He and the trucks are working very hard to make the  look great! The  uses a  to cut the  . He washes the  and cleans all of the machines.

Tonka
Tonka

Finally, a  arrives with the special visitors. The children are here to pick  . Each child gets a  to load up with tasty  .

SCHOOL BUS
Tonka

Now it is time for the  ride!

The  drives through the fields

of  to a  patch. Each

child can take home a  .

Everyone has had a great day

at the  !

Tonka

Did you spot all the picture clues in this book?

Each picture clue is on a flash card. Ask a grown-up to cut out the flash cards. Then try reading the words on the backs of the cards. The pictures will be your clues.

Reading is fun with Tonka!

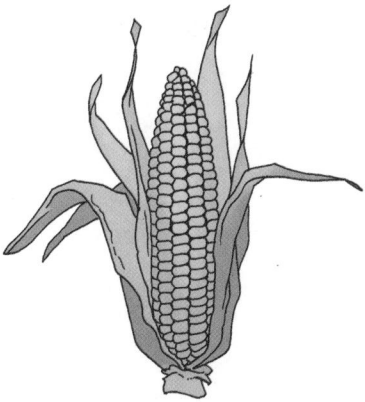

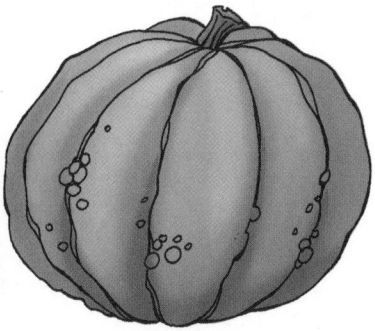

Tonka
Tonka

farmer

farm

corn

apples

pickup truck

pumpkin

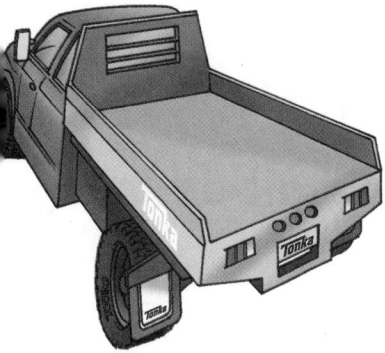
Tonka
Tonka
Tonka

Tonka

trees

flowers

crates

flatbed truck

seeds

tractor

Tonka

forklift

combine harveste

pigs

cow

hay

chicken

Tonka

Tonka

SCHOOL BUS
Tonka
Tonka

baler truck

grass

lawn mower

barn

basket

school bus